The California Raisins™
A Haunting We Will Go!

Written by Mark W. Lewis and developed by
Alchemy II, Inc.

Illustrated by Pat Paris Productions

© 1988 California Raisin Advisory Board
   Licensed by Applause Licensing
   Woodland Hills, CA

Published by Checkerboard Press, a division of Macmillan, Inc.
CHECKERBOARD PRESS and colophon are trademarks of Macmillan, Inc.

Designed by Pat Paris

10 9 8 7 6 5 4 3 2

ISBN 002-688829-7

"Oh man, here comes the rain!" said Tux, as huge raindrops splattered the windshield of The California Raisins' tour bus. The fuel gauge showed empty, so they pulled off the highway and into a gas station in the sleepy little town of Takeanappy.

The gas station attendant began to re-fuel the bus as the Raisins climbed out. "Hey man," asked Tux, "is there a place around here where we can crash for the night?"

"Well...," thought the attendant, "there's always the old Applebee place up on the hill yonder. But some folks say it's haunted!"

"Haunted!" cried Tux.

Just then, a clap of thunder made Hush jump. He whispered something to Tux. "What did he say?" asked the others.

"He says that thunder frightens him," said Tux. Shades slipped up behind Hush and yelled, "Boo!" Hush practically jumped out of his skin and jumped into the bus.

"Hey, man," said Tux. "It isn't cool to scare people."

"C'mon, it was just a joke!" said Sax.

Shades looked around. "Well, why are we standing around here getting damp? Let's go find some dry!"

"Didn't you hear the man? He says the place is haunted!" reminded Spats.

"Aw, c'mon," said Shades, with a laugh. "You're not afraid of a few silly ghosts, are you? Let's go!"

The thunder rolled around them and the attendant shook his head as the bus pulled away.

"I don't think this is a good idea," said Tux, as a flash of lightning lit up the old house in the distance.

Meanwhile, inside the haunted house, all of the ghosts were gathered for a party. The Ghost of Honor was The Shadowy Lady. It was her 300th birthday, and all of her friends had come to celebrate. After the devil's food cake and Boo-berry ice cream, it was time to dance. But when they cranked up the old phonograph, the spring broke! "Now we don't have any music at all!" said The Shadowy Lady.

One of the ghosts heard a noise outside and ran to the window just as the Raisins' bus screeched to a stop. "Oh nooo!" he said. "We have visitors!" They all flocked to the window and watched the Raisins unload and run up to the front door with their instrument cases.

"No one invited them!" said The Shadowy Lady. "How dare they crash my party! We shall have to prepare a very special welcome for them. Everyone get ready!"

With a whirl of sheets and ghostly laughter, all of the spirits vanished into different parts of the house.

The Raisins tried the door, but it wouldn't budge. "It's locked," said Shades.
Hush whispered something to Tux.
"What did he say?" asked Spats.

"He said, 'Good, then we can leave!'" replied Tux. Suddenly the heavy front door creaked and groaned on its hinges and slowly opened before them. "Now I'm *sure* that this is not a good idea," said Spats.

"Follow me!" said Shades bravely, and he strolled into the house. Cautiously, the others entered after him.

It was very dark and scary inside. Hush whispered something hurriedly into Shades' ear. "What did he say?" everyone asked.

"He wants to stay in the bus!" said Shades. But just as Hush turned to run out, the front door slammed shut all by itself! A scary-sounding laugh floated through the house.

"Yeow!" yelped Hush, and he jumped up into Shades' arms.

"Get down, you baby," said Shades. "It was just the wind." He pried Hush off, but Hush jumped back up onto Shades again!

"All right, boys, spread out," said Shades. "We'll see how scary this musty old place is." Each Raisin went in a separate direction except for Hush, who stayed, trembling, to watch the entrance.

Spats went into the dining room to think it all over. He dragged a chair out from the table. But, as he went to sit down, the chair moved out of the way and he plopped down onto the floor! "Hey, that's not funny, you guys!" He turned around, but there was no one there!

"Oh-oh," he said, and hurried back to the entrance.

Sax went up the stairs. Halfway up the second flight, he said, "I'm starved!"
So he sat down on the stairs and pulled a granola bar from his pocket. A small
kitten walked out of the shadows and jumped up into his lap. "Well, hello, little
kitty," said Sax. The kitten sniffed at the granola bar in his hand. "Would you
like a bite?" Just as he said the word "bite," the kitten changed into a giant lion,
opened its mouth really wide and gave a loud *roar*!

"Yeow!!" Sax yelled. He tumbled over backwards down to the first landing. When he stood up again, the lion had vanished. "Oh-oh...!" he said as he turned and ran back toward the entrance.

Tux went into the kitchen. "I'm thirsty," he said, and ran some water from the faucet into a glass. But before he could drink it, the water drained out of the glass all by itself. A scary voice right next to him said, "Yum—delicious!"

"Oh-oh..." said Tux. "I'm outta here!" And he took off running!

Shades was walking down the long, dark hallway. He was getting less bold with every step. "I wonder what's in here?" he thought as he came to a closet at the end of the hall. When he opened the door, there was The Shadowy Lady herself!

"Go away!" she shouted in a ghostly voice. Shades turned pale, yelled "Mommy!" and ran as fast as he could with the ghost right behind him! He wasn't very brave now!

All of the Raisins collided in the entryway and fell in a frightened heap. The ghosts were closing in! The Shadowy Lady hovered over them and shouted, "You have ruined my party!"

"Party?" asked Tux.

"Yes, and you have spoiled it!" she said.

"Hey man, like, what's a party without music?" added Sax.

Hush whispered something to Sax who pulled out his saxaphone and started to play. Spats got up and began to jive to the music.

The Shadowy Lady stopped and listened. The music was so good, she started to tap her foot. The other Raisins hopped up and pulled out their instruments. In a moment, the old house was filled with the hip music of The California Raisins! All of the ghosts came and the party *really* started.

The next morning, The California Raisins waved goodbye to the ghosts and The Shadowy Lady. "It just goes to show that music really is the best way to make friends," said Spats.

"I saw you guys," said Shades. "You were really scared in there."

"So were you," said Sax.

"What, me? Humpf! Nothin' scares me!" boasted Shades as he adjusted his shades. Suddenly he jumped and yelled as a big, black spider dropped down in front of his eyes! "Yeow!!"

Hush pulled the paper spider back over the edge of the seat and they all laughed as they drove off down the road.